My Queen

By Peter "Wolfie" Wolfinger

MY QUEEN

1210 SW 23rd PL • Ocala, FL 34471 • Phone 352-622-1825
Website: www.atlantic-pub.com • Email: sales@atlantic-pub.com
SAN Number: 268-1250

Library of Congress Control Number: 2022915859

Printed in the United States

PROJECT MANAGER: Crystal Edwards
INTERIOR LAYOUT AND JACKET DESIGN: Nicole Sturk

Dedication

This book is dedicated to all the women and men who have served in the military, signing a blank check to protect our freedom, and especially to my family.

Rudolph Wolfinger	Civil War
Michael Wolfinger	WWI
Charles Wolfinger	WWII
Joseph Wolfinger	WWII
Charles Wolfinger	Vietnam
Peter Wolfinger	Vietnam Desert storm Iraqi freedom

Table of Contents

Acknowledgments vii

Prologue ix

His Penthouse 1

Secret Room 3

Candy.. 5

Four Years Later They Meet Again 21

Six Months Later 27

Crystal 35

Three Months Later... 49

The Request.. 53

London... 57

The Queen's Ball 83

Russia...91

Conclusion.. 93

To My Sisters and Brothers of the Military 97

This is My Story.. 99

Acknowledgments

While this is my third book, my acknowledgments will always be the same. While not a religious person, I do believe in God and angels, and it's because of them I have lived this long.

I would like to thank our Lord for allowing me to live long enough to write this story. I'm sure that when I go home, He will give me a bill for a chiropractor for the many times He has carried me throughout my life.

Many thanks to my wife and my friends for their support. And to *Alexa* for all the times I have asked her to spell a word.

Another special thanks to Crystal Edwards and her team at Atlantic Publishing Group. They believed in my manuscript and helped this dream come true.

Last but not least, thanks to life. We do not realize how precious life is until we are about to lose it.

Prologue

This is the story of a young man named Peter Wolfinger who grew up in Fort Lauderdale, Florida. He was the youngest of his siblings, and his family owned a five-star hotel on the beach. His parents, Sophia and Charles, managed the hotel while his brother Charles Junior and sister-in-law Connie ran the five-star restaurant, "Josephine", located inside the hotel. His sister Joanne was a doctor and kept an office in the hotel, while her husband Jerry oversaw the poker room.

The hotel was named "The Hotel Wolfinger," and was built in the 1930s by Pete's ancestor. Nobody really knows where he got the money, but no expense was spared. The hotel has 120 rooms, with each floor holding ten suites and one penthouse. There remains ample indoor and outdoor parking, at least 15 high-end stores and six professional offices on the main floor, all while maintaining an indoor and outdoor pool, a sauna, bowling alley, and a poker room. It even had a helicopter pad. The hotel was known for providing every amenity known.

The hotel stands 12 stories tall and each family member had a penthouse. The grandparents had the penthouse on the 12th floor, which was said to have a secret room that nobody ever found, including his grandparents. Pete was 15 at the time his grandparents passed, and Pete's father became heartbroken from it, closing up the penthouse, allowing nobody to live in it.

Pete and his good friend Joseph were childhood buddies, lifting weights and studying karate together since the age of 7. When they graduated high school at the age of 17, they asked permission from their parents to join the Army. They applied for Green Beret training and were accepted. The program took one year, and they both graduated at the age of 18. Their first assignment was a tour in Afghanistan (also known as Sandpit), returning home at the age of 19.

His Penthouse

After dropping Joe off at his parents' house, Pete got out of the cab and entered the hotel. His whole family was there to meet him and welcome him home, and after all the hugging and kissing, his parents asked if they could talk to him in the family dining room. Once everyone was seated, Pete's father stood up and said, "Pete, we all got together and agreed that it's time you have your own penthouse. We also agreed that since you were the last to be brought up by your grandparents, you can have their penthouse should you wish. The condition is the same as it is for the rest of us: the penthouse is your responsibility; if you want to do anything, you have to pay for it. When you're home, the maintenance is $1,000 a month, which will cover the daily maid service and utilities, and I mean just the maid service — nothing else."

Everybody laughed.

"When you're not there, it will drop down to $500 a month. Your mother removed everything that was personal. All the bedding and linens have been changed. What do you say?"

Pete replied, "I can't thank you enough. I truly feel blessed to have such a family. Thank you, and I look forward to having my own place with my family."

When Pete entered the penthouse that was once his grandparents, he could smell his grandfather's cherry pipe tobacco, and his grandmother's perfume, *Windsong*, hit him strongly. He started to feel pain in his heart because he missed them. As he walked through the penthouse reminiscing on growing up there, he reviewed what he would like to change. There really was not much — maybe a bigger TV in the sitting area. But one thing you could say about his grandparents was that they always kept up with everything. The penthouse consisted of a library, small gym, laundry room, kitchen, dining room, a large sitting area with a seaside view, and four bedrooms with two master suites. As he looked around, he could not be happier.

Secret Room

*P*ete's next step was to see if he could find that secret room everybody talked about. Nobody knew where it was, and after reviewing the whole penthouse, Pete felt that it had to be somewhere in the library. As he walked through the library, he looked around very carefully, seeing the whole room had wall-to-wall bookcases but not noticing anything that would suggest a hidden room. He looked closely at the trim that separated the bookcases and noticed that one bookcase had the trim but it was nailed on only one side, allowing it to slide behind the other bookcase. He tried sliding the bookcase, but when it didn't move, he tried pushing it in and out to no avail. He scoured the bookcases and noticed that there was a bust of George Washington on the adjacent shelf. He walked over to the bust, looked at it very carefully, and noticed a slight crack underneath the hairline. He tried lifting the hair up, and there was a button. He pressed the button and the bookshelf slid to the left, exposing a small 10x10 room. He used the light from his iPhone and was able to see the room, where there was a desk, chair, and a shelf with ledgers. On the desk, there were small envelopes that had names, hours, and amounts printed on them, with a very comfortable looking chair and a small safe beside it. He noticed a wall switch. He turned on it and a couple lights in the ceiling lit. He noticed air vents high in the ceiling. Pete figured this room had to have been built during the construction of the hotel.

Pete called his father and told him the exciting news, but his father's response was not what he expected.

His father said, "Tell no one, and forget about the safe. This way it will truly be a secret room."

Not understanding why his father said that, he chose to respect his father's wishes, agreeing to tell no one.

Candy

*P*ete got off the elevator, thinking about how fast his leave had gone by. *At least I have five days left*, he thought until he heard crying in front of the registration desk. He looked over and noticed a young girl with red hair, about five foot four, with a nice figure, looking sad. People walked by her shaking their heads. Pete walked over and asked, "Are you all right?"

She looked up at him with sad blue eyes, saying, "Somebody stole my money, and my car won't start. All of the hotels around here are full because there are a lot of conventions happening. Now I'm caught in the rain. I have no place to stay, and I'm supposed to try out for the American talent show tomorrow." After this, she just sat down on the floor and cried.

Pete called over the night clerk, Sharon, and asked if this was true.

Sharon replied, "Yes, we have no rooms."

Pete asked the young girl, "What's your name?"

Shivering, she replied, "My name is Candy."

Pete asked, "Do you have a last name?"

She said, "Yes, but don't make fun of me . . . it's Cotton."

Pete then asked, "Do you have a license?"

Candy replied affirmatively and showed it to him, asking, "What is with all the questions?"

Pete replied, "I may be able to help you. I have a penthouse with four bedrooms. Three are empty, you could stay in one as long as you like. I'll be leaving Friday, and you can have the whole penthouse to yourself. The only condition is, please do not bring any males up to the penthouse. You look cold, please stand up."

Pete took off his jacket, exposing his very well musculed body, wrapping it around Candy. A few girls passing by whistled, and Pete just smiled.

Candy said, "I will not give you sex."

And Pete replied, "That's okay."

Candy said, "Then why are you helping me?"

Pete replied, "Because everyone needs help at one time or another, and I enjoy helping people when I can. Excuse me, I have to make a call. I'll be right back."

As he walked away, Sharon leaned over the counter and said "Are you crazy? Girls would line up to give him sex!"

Candy said, "I don't care! I will not give him sex that way."

At that moment, Pete returned, saying to Sharon, "Please call Greg and ask him to pick up Candy's car. Candy, please give the keys to Sharon. Are you hungry, Candy?"

Candy replied with a nod.

Pete replied, "Great! My family and I are about to have dinner, and you are welcome to come with me. I'm sure everyone will enjoy your company as you will theirs."

As they entered the dining room, Candy noticed two empty chairs. Candy now knew why Pete walked away and made a telephone call after the introductions. As everybody sat down, Mr. W said the dinner prayer before eating. They mainly spoke about the running of the hotel and they never ask Candy personal questions. After dinner, Candy and Pete left for his penthouse.

In the elevator, Candy said, "I want you to know my past."

Pete replied, "I'm not asking."

But Candy said, "Well, I'm telling you anyway. I never knew my father. My mother died of alcoholism. I lived with my grandmother, who had nothing. When she also passed, I figured I had nothing to lose, and people say I have a good voice so I headed this way to try out for this contest."

As they entered the penthouse, Candy said, "Wow, this is beautiful, but I'm not giving you sex."

Pete smiled. "I will survive. You can pick any bedroom. The best one is the other master opposite mine. There is a lock, and there is food and water in the fridge." Pete showed Candy the bedroom and said, "Let's get up about 4:40 a.m., there may be a lot of people that want the same thing you want. You have everything you need in the bedroom, so please feel free to use them. See you tomorrow."

At 4:40 am, Pete knocked on Candy's door. Candy slid the door open and said, "Good morning."

Pete replied, "Good morning," while looking at what she was wearing. Pete said, "You can't wear that outfit."

Candy said, "Why?"

Pete replied, "Because your ladies are ready to pop out, and your shorts look like they are part of your body."

She replied, "I have nothing else to wear."

Pete said, "Be right back," and went into his room before coming out with one of his shirts. "Here, you should be able to wear this like a dress if you put a belt around it. And here is a necklace with an arrowhead I used to wear when I was a kid."

Candy went into her bedroom to change. When she came out, she looked very pretty.

Pete gave her a bag and said, "It contains two bottles of water, some power bars, and a throw away poncho. Here is $100 for registration."

Candy started crying and said, "I feel so bad."

Pete replied, "Don't feel bad. I'm sure when you get on your feet, you'll pay me back. Don't worry about it now. Let's go to my car and hit the road to the show."

They both laughed as they headed for the garage.

Pete took the car cover off and Candy couldn't stop laughing. She said, "Are you sure your car will run?"

Pete replied, "Yes, I built the engine myself. Someday I'm going to have this car off the frame, which means that when I get it back, it will be like brand new."

As Candy entered the car, she asked, "Why is there duct tape on the seats? Why is there a grip lock plier on the handle? Why are there different colors on the car?"

Pete replied, "I put this car together while I was in high school with spare parts that I bought with my own money, and someday I will take my baby to a shop where it will be taken off the frame and every part will be redone. It will be painted metal flake green with a saddle interior, the car will look like it came out of the showroom."

Candy replied, "Well, I think that is an excellent idea and I hope it comes true for you".

Pete was waiting for Candy by the car when he saw her waving the ticket as she ran past two young men. One of the men smacked her on her backside, laughing. The man asked, "Did you like that?"

Candy turned and tried hitting him in the face, but he was too tall, so he grabbed her hands and held them while trying to lift her dress up, laughing while saying, "What are you going to do now?"

Before he could lift up Candy's dress, Pete was there. He broke the first guy's nose. The second guy let Candy go and started to swing at Pete, but Pete blocked his swing and hit the guy in the stomach. Then you could hear his jaw bone crack.

Pete turned to Candy and said, "Go wait in the car. I'll be right there."

Candy nodded with tears coming down her eyes, and Pete then turned to the two guys laying on the ground and said, "If I ever catch you in Fort Lauderdale again, you will end up much worse."

Candy and Pete arrived at Greg's garage just as Greg was shutting the hood on Candy's car. Greg saw Pete and smiled. He said, "Long time no see."

Pete replied, "Same here." After introducing Candy, he said, "The car belongs to the young lady — what's the damage?"

Greg replied, "Well, the car is not worth saving. The engine is shot and the tires are bald, and it needs new brakes. The best I could do is offer you $500 for junk if you want it."

Candy looked at Pete.

Pete said, "It's your call, Candy. I will back you whatever you want to do."

Candy said to Greg, "I'll take the money." So they went into the office and signed the papers.

When they got into Pete's car, Candy said, "I don't know what I'm going to do without a car."

Pete said, "You won't need one because you're going to win the golden ticket, then fly to California."

Smiling, she said, "I sure hope so. What do you say we go to Walmart and I get some clothes that fit me?"

As they were walking into Walmart, they saw a firetruck out front giving out literature on fire hazards.

Candy said, "I'm going to go look in the ladies' department, do you want to come?"

Pete said, "I'll pass. I'm going to go look in the toy department. Remember, little boys don't grow up, but the price of the toys do."

They both laughed and went their separate ways. Pete was looking in the model section, hoping to find the model of his 1970 442 Oldsmobile. While looking, he noticed a stuffed bear that was made of all different colors.

Pete thought, *Wow, the bear looks like candy colors, this would be a great gift for Candy, and may even cheer her up.*

After paying for their merchandise, they walked through the front door only to notice that the fire department was around Pete's car. Pete and Candy ran over to his car, only to see that the inside of the car was burnt. He turned to the fire chief and said, "What happened?"

The fire chief said, "Those two guys over there threw a fire bomb in your car! Lucky we were here, so you didn't get much damage."

Pete and Candy started walking over to the sheriff, and as they got closer, they recognized the two men as the men Pete fought earlier that day. They explained to the sheriff what had happened, and told them that they believed that was why the two guys retaliated by throwing a fire bomb in his car.

The sheriff said, "Do you want to press charges?"

Pete said, "No," and as he walked away, Pete called Greg, telling him what happened and asked if he would pick up his car. He kept it in his yard for a while promising Greg that he would pay him $100 a month till he could get the car repaired, and Greg said it was no problem. Pete then called a cab to take them back to the hotel.

Once in the penthouse, Pete said, "Candy, we really had a busy day, and you look beat. Why don't you go rest for a while?"

Candy replied, "That sounds like a great idea. I was up half the night worrying if I would get a ticket."

Candy woke up about 11 p.m., and she looked around. Seeing that everything was dark, she got out of bed, walked into the great room, and while she didn't see Pete, she did notice a light coming through the bottom of the door on the other end of the penthouse. As she walked towards the light, she heard the clanging of metal. She was just able to see between the door and the wall, and saw Pete lifting weights. His body was glistening with sweat, his muscles bulging from the strain. Candy stood watching him for about ten minutes and found herself getting excited. She quietly turned around and went back to her bedroom, hoping her batteries were not dead.

The following morning Candy woke up to the smell of bacon and coffee, which made her very hungry. She quickly got out of bed, took a quick shower, got dressed, and went to the kitchen where she saw Pete cooking.

When Pete saw her, he said, "Good morning, sleepyhead. Have a good sleep?"

Candy replied, "Yes, best sleep I've had in a long time."

Pete smile and said, "Are you hungry? I've got bacon and eggs waiting for you."

Candy replied, "Oh, yes. I'm very hungry."

Pete said, "Great! And after breakfast, let's go to the Riverwalk. This is our last free day, since tomorrow you get your golden ticket and Friday morning I leave."

Candy felt sad. When Pete said he was leaving, she mentioned, "Any chance you can stay and come with me?"

Pete looked at her, smiled, and said, "I don't think my boss would like that."

They got back from the Riverwalk just in time for dinner with the family. The family was very supportive of Candy, wishing her all the luck in the world and telling her that she would definitely get the golden ticket. Candy thanked everyone, and after dinner, Candy and Pete went back up to the penthouse to spend the night of leisure.

As they were sitting out on the balcony having a drink, Candy turned to Pete and said, "How come you never tried to have sex with me?"

Smiling, Pete replied, "Remember? You said no sex."

Candy said, "Not everyone woman means what they say." Candy got up and said, "I'm going to bed. I'll see you tomorrow. I have to be there about 10 a.m."

Pete replied, "Okay, no problem. Goodnight, Candy."

And Candy went in, wishing she had a door to slam.

The next morning, Pete had breakfast waiting for her. When she got to the table, she looked at Pete, smiling, and said, "Thank you. I'm sorry about last night."

Pete replied, "Don't worry, Candy. It's okay."

Candy said, "You've never heard me sing. Why do you have so much faith in me?"

Pete replied, "Because, Candy, I believe in you. And when you believe in a person, you shouldn't question it. Let's go get the golden ticket."

Candy came through the swinging doors waving a golden ticket saying, "I got it! *I got it!*" As she rushed towards Pete and got closer, she jumped up, putting her arms around Pete's neck.

Then she wrapped her legs around his waist, giving him a kiss that would make any man envious.

Pete gently put her down, saying, "That's great, Candy. Now let's go home and tell the family."

By the time Candy filled out all the paperwork, found a cab, and made it back to the hotel, it was dinner time. When Candy and Pete walked into the family dining room, everybody stood up and clapped. Candy started to cry for all the love everyone was showing her.

After dinner, Pete told everyone at the table that they were going to meet his friend Joe and his date to celebrate. "All are welcome."

Everyone at the table declined, saying that it was for young people.

Pete's mother said, "You will say so long before you leave?"

Pete walked over to his mother and hugged her while telling her, "I would never leave without saying so long to my mom."

The night went fast and before they knew it, it was midnight.

Joe said, "I'm going to leave," reminding Pete not to forget that they had to get up early the next day.

Pete said, "Thanks for reminding me, my friend."

After Joe and his girlfriend left, Candy said, "Why don't you call your boss and tell him you won't be in?"

Pete looked at Candy and smiled while saying, "We don't have a nice boss. Let's go — we're both a little tipsy already, so I might be late whether I want to be or not."

After they entered the penthouse, they kicked off their shoes, enjoying the view of the ocean and the beautiful full moon shining on the water while they walked down towards their bedrooms.

Candy said, "This is a really gorgeous night."

When they were in front of Candy's bedroom, Candy gently took Pete's hand and pulled him towards her while pulling him toward the bedroom.

Pete reluctantly pulled back, saying, "Candy, we really shouldn't be doing this."

Candy said, "I want to," as she pushed him onto the bed while taking his shirt off. Candy unbuttoned her shirt dress, and smiling, she said, "I don't want to give your shirt back." Candy stood naked in front of Pete. She gently pushed Pete back on the bed while pulling down his shorts. She kissed him on his stomach, working up to his neck. She said, "I truly want you."

Pete felt her breasts on his chest as she reached down, gently sliding his manhood into her. As they kissed, both went into a world just for them, climaxing at the same time. Then, Candy gently rolled off Pete and laid by his side, wrapping her arms around him as they fell asleep.

Pete's internal alarm woke him at 4:30 in the morning, this time with a hangover. Feeling a warm body next to him, he looked over and saw Candy sleeping. He got up quietly, picked up his clothes, went into his bedroom, took a nice cold shower, and dressed in his uniform. He was leaving his bedroom when he saw Candy standing in front of him.

Candy said, "Are you one of those funny soldiers?"

Pete replied, "I've been called many things, but never that."

Candy said, "You know what I mean, like the Rambo guy."

Pete laughed, saying, "Do you mean Green Beret Special Forces?"

Candy replied, "Yes, and how come you never told me?"

Pete said, "Would it have made a difference?"

Candy replied, "We won't know now, because you never told me." Candy started to cry, saying, "Did you plan on leaving without saying so long, too?"

Pete replied, "No, I was just going over to your room to wake you. I wanted to let you know that you could use my place as long as you want. But no men. There's an envelope on the table with $2,000 in it."

Candy said, "I can't take it."

Pete replied "It's not a gift — it's a loan. When you get to be that superstar we know you will be, you can give it back."

When they got to the front door, Pete turned to kiss Candy, saying, "Take care of yourself."

Candy said, "When are you coming back?"

Pete just shrugged his shoulders.

Candy shut the door, and she never felt so alone as she walked to his bedroom, took one of his shirts, and put it to her face while lying down on his bed, and cried herself to sleep.

Four Years Later
They Meet Again

*I*t was early Christmas Eve morning when Pete entered his penthouse. As he walked towards his bedroom, he heard noises coming from the other master bedroom. He looked in the bedroom, and saw Candy. Pete held out his arms, and said, "Hello, stranger."

Candy turned towards the voice. When she saw Pete, she jumped up, exclaiming, "You're home!" as she ran to him.

After hugging and kissing each other, Pete said, "Give me a few moments so I can change."

Candy followed him into the bedroom.

Smiling, Pete turned and said, "I read that you are going to be a married woman soon."

Laughing, Candy replied, "Yes, I know, but I've already seen you naked, and I just want to know if you still have those tight abs."

Pete smiled, took off his shirt, then asked, "Are the abs still the same?"

Candy replied, "Yes," then noticed his shoulder and asked what had happened.

Pete replied, "I should've zigged instead of zagged. Got hit."

Candy started to cry.

He walked over to her and hugged her, saying, "Don't cry. I'm okay — it's just a scar."

Just then, they heard a young voice saying, "Mommy, where are you?"

Candy responded, "I'm in here with Uncle Pete."

The little boy ran to where his mother's voice was coming, with his nanny right behind him. When he got to his mother, he looked up to Pete.

Pete held out his hand and said, "My name is Uncle Pete. What's yours?"

The young boy replied, "Pete James Johnson." He then turned to his mother and said, "We can't get into Legoland. Maria said the park is full and will not allow anyone else in."

Pete said, "Let's see if Uncle Pete can help." He took out his phone and called his brother Charlie. "Hi Charlie . . . Yes, I'm home . . . Yes, Mom and Dad know. Listen, do you still know the bigshot in Legoland? . . . You do? How about calling him and seeing if we can get five tickets to get in today? . . . Yes, I'll hang on . . . Great! Thanks, brother! Tell him we will be there in 20 minutes."

Pete said, "All right, let's go!"

Candy said to Maria, "Please take Pete James to the front door. We will be there in a few minutes."

After they left, Pete said to Candy, "You know, I will marry you."

Candy replied, "It wouldn't work. Besides, I'm getting married in two weeks."

Pete started to say, "Is he —"

But Candy stopped him, saying, "Don't go there. Now, let me fix my makeup, and I will meet you by the front door."

Once everyone was together, Pete said, "Should I call a cab?"

Candy said, "No, since we have a car in the garage, we'll take that."

The garage elevator door opened, and Pete asked, "Where to?"

Candy said, "Over to the right — the one with the cover on it."

Pete walked over to the car, pulled the cover off, and he stood still, staring at the car.

Candy said, "Merry Christmas! Do you like it? I tried to get it the way you wanted it."

Pete turned towards Candy, his eyes moist, saying, "The car is perfect — like you." He then picked her up and kissed her.

Pete James said, "I'm telling my daddy!"

Pete said, "I gave your mommy a thank you kiss. Now it is your turn!" He picked Pete James up and kissed him on both cheeks while saying, "Thank you." Then Pete said, "Let's not leave Maria out!" and he kissed her.

At the dinner table, Pete James was falling asleep at the table, so Candy excused herself, saying it is time to put Pete James to bed.

Pete stayed behind so he could converse with his family. After a while, Pete said, "It has been a long day. I'm calling it a night. See everyone tomorrow for breakfast." So he went upstairs to his penthouse.

As Pete was walking to his bedroom, he saw Candy out on the balcony with two wine glasses and a bottle of wine. As he got closer, Candy said, "Join me for a nightcap?"

Pete replied, "Why not?" He sat down, saying to Candy, "Well, tell me all about the love of your life."

Candy smiled and said "I love him as much as I love you. He is a veteran, spent six years in the Coast Guard, and he owns a construction business."

Pete replied, "Then that is good enough for me."

Just then, Pete's phone rang. "Excuse me," Pete said as he got up to answer the phone. Pete stood there and said, "Yes . . . Immediately, sir . . . I hear the helicopter now . . . Yes, sir. Joe will meet me down there."

Pete turned to Candy and said, "I have to leave," and he went into his bedroom and started to change into his camouflage clothing.

Candy stood there stunned and said, "It's Christmas Eve."

Pete replied, "War does not have holidays. I have to leave now."

Candy started to cry.

Pete hugged her and said "Don't cry — we'll meet again." Pete took his pin off his dress uniform and handed it to Candy, saying, "Merry Christmas, Candy. I don't have much, but this is my most prized possession. Wear it proudly."

Six Months Later

Candy and her secretary, Lori Bean, entered the limo. Major Teresa Vasquez was sitting in the limo.

"Good morning," Teresa said, and they replied the same. Major Vasquez said, "Thank you for your kindness and for seeing our wounded soldiers."

Candy replied, "It is an honor. Who will we be seeing today?"

Major Vasquez said, "This is a unique group of Green Berets." Immediately, Candy's face started to get pale, as the major read the list of names:

Weapons Sergeant Ed Addeo; wife, Lynn

Weapons Sergeant Vito Vavallo; wife, Phyllis

Medical Sergeant Wayne Ward; single

Communication Sergeant Tony Monte; single

Warrant Officer Joseph Perrette; single

Captain Pete Wolfinger; single

Candy went white and tears started running down her cheeks.
The major looked up from her paperwork, and seeing that
Candy was crying, she said, "Are you all right?"

Candy replied, "Yes, Major. Thank you. Do you know the condition of Pete Wolfinger and how it happened?"

The major looked at her papers, saying, "All it says is that he is
alive, but I could read the statement from the warrent officer if
you want?"

Candy replied, "Please."

The following is a statement given by Warrant Officer Joseph
Perrette no. RA 00556. Interviewer Captain Canto of the United
States Army.

Mr. Perrette stated the following:

> *On February 17, 2022, Captain Pete Wolfinger came to our
> barracks and asked for volunteers to go on an unauthorized
> mission, objective: to kill Abul Hannan Aklthar, the leader of
> the Taliban. We all volunteered, and prepared to leave that
> day at midnight, packing plenty of ammo.*
>
> *We were about five miles into enemy territory when we de-
> cided to rest behind some boulders for protection. The cap-
> tain viewed what was ahead and he stated it looks like flat
> land the size of a football field, which meant that we would
> be in the open, before we could get to any cover, the captain*

turned to his K-9, Bear, and said, 'Be on guard,' then we started to move forward.

We were about a half a football field across when the Taliban came out behind the rocks opposite us. We were both startled, both of us started firing at once because we were so close. Both sides were taking casualties, and the captain yelled, 'Fall back!'

A sand storm then appeared, making it hard for both sides to see. But everyone kept firing, and Pete's team was well trained; if one team member yelled hit, the other team members knew by the voice who it was. Pete would run to the team member and pick him up and carry him to cover, while firing his own weapon. The last one was Joe, and after all the members were behind the boulders, the sand storm stopped.

It felt like God had sent help. Each member was helping another member when a voice from the enemy hollered, 'Captain, are you there? I am Abul Hannan Aklthar — the leader of the Taliban. I speak good English, yes? I learned in your country and was even paid to do so — nice country.'

Pete said, 'What is it that you want?'

Abul replied, 'You are a very hard man to kill. I know you caught my spy and he told you that I wanted to attack your compound, kidnap your famous Candy, and make her my slave. I know you know her, Captain. I know that is why you are here. I'll propose that just you and I fight to the death. I know your reinforcements will be here in two hours, but I have enough men to overrun yours now.'

I said to Pete, 'This guy is nuts — do you think you can even trust him?'

Pete said, 'Look around — everyone is wounded.' Pete said to Abul, 'What are the terms?'

Abul said, 'We must all give our word that we will not fire at each other. My men swear to Allah. When I kill you, I will not attack your men.'

Pete said, 'What if I kill you?'

Abul laughed, saying, 'That is not possible, but should it be, I will give you nine European slaves, my men will withdraw, we will not attack the compound, and your men will live.'

Pete said to me, 'Promise me if I lose, you will shoot him.'

I said, 'But we all gave our word.'

Pete said, 'Since when do you keep your word?'

I said to Pete. 'If I do, they will overrun us.'

Pete said, 'Then take a vote.'

The team agreed to shoot him if Pete lost. I said to Pete, 'Don't lose.'

Pete said, 'Abul, you step out first,' which he did.

He looked like he just came out of a genie bottle, bare-chested, muscular, about 6'4", 230 pounds, and holding a weird looking knife.

When Pete stepped out, Abul showed surprised that Pete was just as muscular and tall.

They walk towards each other until they were about four feet apart, and they said something, but I couldn't hear. They circled each other, but then it was like a blur. Abul cut Pete across the chest, and Pete cut Abul across the face, which seemed to piss him off. He charged Pete, and in doing so, left his front open. I believe he realized too late that Pete was left-handed. Pete put his knife into Abul, causing Abul to drop his knife and try to keep Pete from going deeper. It didn't work. Once he fell, Pete looked straight at the boulders that the enemy was hiding behind. Then he turned, walked over to Bear, picked him up, and started walking back to us when the enemy threw a bomb. It exploded, pieces of shrapnel hitting the captain in the back, and before we could even fire, an enemy soldier ran out from behind the boulder, crying and waving his hands up in the air, when one of his own shot him.

A voice behind him said, 'The captives are coming out now.' The next thing I know, we are here and you are asking me questions.

"Captain Canto asked, 'Is there anything else you wish to add?' Joe said, 'No.'" Major Vazquez looked up from her paperwork and said to Candy, "At least we know what happened."

Candy replied, "What will happen to them?"

The major said, "Unless the colonel changes his tune, they will be given the medals they deserve and then be court martialed."

The car pulled up in front of the hospital, and Candy said to the major, "I have to go to the ladies' room before I meet these brave men."

Candy looked inside the ward, seeing the men lying in their beds, and she tried not to cry. But the tears came, and she wiped them away and walked in, spending about fifteen minutes with every man, thanking them for their bravery. When she got to Joe, Candy said, "How are you feeling, Joe?"

He replied, "Good."

Candy noticed Joe was staring at her chest. She smiled and said, "It hasn't been that long, has it?"

Joe blushed and said, "I was looking at the signature pin you are wearing — it looks like Pete's."

Candy replied, "Pete gave it to me. Why do you ask?"

Joe replied that pin was worn by his grandfather who served in Vietnam, his father who served in Desert Storm, and his brother who served in Iraq.

Candy said "I'm going to take good care of it. Where is he?"

Joe replied, "In the room across the hall, but prepare yourself."

Candy ran across the hall to the room and opened the door. When she saw Pete, she fainted, and the nurse and doctor gently placed her in a chair. When she woke up, she looked over at Pete, who was in a coma with tubes going into him.

She started to turn pale, and the doctor said, "Maybe you should leave."

Candy said, "No, I'm okay," as she got up and walked over to the bed. Candy turned and said, "Can I please have a few moments alone? Thank you."

After everyone left the room, she took his hand, saying "Pete, while I don't understand what your love means to me, I do know I love you with all my heart just like I love my husband and family. I hope someday you do find true love, and get a chance to meet my husband, James, and our daughters. Pete James is growing like a weed, so hurry up and get well."

Candy bent over and kissed him and removed her hand. She felt Pete squeeze it lightly. She started to cry as she walked away, and once outside, she asked to be taken back to her hotel.

Once in the hotel, Candy said, "Lori, please bring me my checkbook." Candy said, "I'm going to write out a check for $2 million dollars for each man. Please send a bottle of my perfume to their wives and contact my accountant, Liva Brong, and find out how we can give the money to them tax-free. Then call General Ronald Keeling, and please let me know when you have him on the phone."

Moments later, Lori said, "He's on the phone, Mrs. Johnson."

Candy thanked her, saying, "Hello, General . . . Yes, that's very nice of you . . . Yes, thank you. I'm calling you to let you know about the colonel who thinks the men that you recently gave medals to went out on a mission without his approval. I believe he made a mistake, because he did give his approval. And if you can't correct this misinformation, I'll put it in the paper tomorrow . . . Yes, I know . . . Okay, you have the rest of the day to straighten this out. If not, it goes in the paper . . . Thank you, General. I knew I could count on you." She hung up.

Candy said to Lori, "Sometimes I have to pinch myself to ensure I'm awake since I'm so blessed to have started out broke and am now worth $600 million."

Crystal

*P*ete sat at the table in his brother's restaurant looking out the window and thinking how thankful he was that Cathie and Olivia were excellent therapists. With their help, he was able to get back 100 percent of his mobility after his injuries. This now helped him pass his physical to stay in the Army. Needless to say, it felt great when he came home. The family was waiting for him, finally getting a chance to meet Candy's husband, James, the girls, and Pete James again.

He was thinking about all of this when he noticed a tall, pretty, and young brunette with a gentleman entering the restaurant. He could see their reflection in the window as they were being seated. He noticed the young lady look towards him and smile as the waitress came over. They ordered drinks, and then the young lady got up and left. Pete noticed the gentleman put something in the young lady's drink. When she came back, she sat down, and while talking, she was about to take a sip of her drink.

Pete stood up and started walking over to the table, saying, "I wouldn't drink that."

She looked up at Pete, saying, "Why?"

Pete replied, "Because that gentleman put something in your drink."

And the gentlemen said, "No, I didn't. Why are you starting trouble?"

Pete took the glass, put it in front of the gentlemen, and said, "Then you drink it."

The gentlemen replied, "I will not. How dare you cause trouble? If you don't leave, I will call the police."

Pete replied, "Go ahead. I'll wait."

The gentleman looked at the young lady and said, "I'm sorry, Crystal. It was just a slight knockout drug. Your family friend, Ken, doesn't want you to go the meeting tomorrow."

Crystal said, "What meeting, Stan?"

Stan replied, "Ken is having some gambling issues and the gambling boss said that he wants Ken to sell his shares to him. If he does, he will wipe his debt clean."

Crystal replied, "I can't believe this. Ken knows he cannot sell the shares for a year — it's only been six months! His share has already made $100,000 on his initial profit."

Stan replied, "Well, they're going to do everything to stop you from going to the meeting, because if you don't show up, then he can sell the shares to whomever he wants. That's in the contract, right?"

Crystal said, "Yes, but I never thought he would stoop to this level."

Stan said, "Well, those two guys outside are there to make sure you're not going to come to the meeting. I understand they have men in front of your sister's house, your parents' house, Aunt Margaret's house, and your family's building. They're not taking any chances on you showing up."

Pete said to Stan, "Okay, leave."

Stan got up, saying, "Remember what I said, Crystal."

As he left the building, Crystal said, "I don't know what to do."

Pete replied, "If you're willing to trust me, I can help. Do you trust me?"

Crystal looked into his eyes and said, "I do."

Pete then took her hand, said to follow him, and they went through the restaurant and kitchen to the freight elevator. They took the freight elevator up to the 12th floor. As the doors of the elevator opened, Pete said to Crystal, "Are you afraid dogs?"

They entered Pete's penthouse, and Crystal said, "No."

Just then, Bear barked, and Crystal was frightened, and hugged Pete. She said, "He looks like a real bear!"

Pete laughed and said to Bear, "Give Crystal your paw," which Bear did, "Now go lie down." Pete said, "Would you like something to drink while we talk?"

Crystal said, "Water, please." Crystal told Pete about her company and her plans to expand then sell to the highest bidder.

Pete said, "I like that idea. You have a good head on your shoulders. May I ask why you don't go to your parents?"

Crystal replied, "My family owns Edwards Import and Export Co., one of the largest in the world, but I want to build my own empire."

Pete said, "I truly like your plan. If you let me, I will give you the money to buy out Ken."

Crystal replied, "I need a cashier's check to wave in front of his face."

Pete said, "Don't worry about that," and he picked up the phone and called the family banker. He told him he wanted a certified check for $620,000 by the end of the night.

Crystal said, "I'm impressed, but I'm not giving you sex."

Pete replied, "I've been hearing that a lot lately from women I first meet — must be my underarm deodorant."

They both laughed, and Crystal said "I don't mix business with pleasure, but once our business is done, we will have pleasure. How am I going to get past the bodyguards?"

Pete replied, "Give me a moment." He called the Bellboy Tom, then asked, "Will you please go to Walmart and pick up a baseball cap, extra-large sweatshirt, size-medium jogging pants, and a pair of size 9 sneakers? When you come back, I'll reimburse you and give you a generous tip."

Crystal said, "How did you know my shoe size?"

Pete replied, "Lucky guess. Well, everything you need is in the guest room. What do you say we get a good night's sleep, and I'll see you tomorrow 7a.m.?"

Crystal replied, "Sounds like a plan to me. Goodnight."

The next morning, Crystal and Pete left for the Edwards building by hailing a cab. Right as the cab arrived, Pete handed him a $50 bill and told him to keep the change and to stop right before the Edwards building.

Pete got out and told Crystal, "No matter what happens, do not look back at me." Pete waited for the cab to get in front of the Edwards building, and when Crystal got out and went into the front door, Pete followed, staying just a few feet behind her, making it look like they were strangers. As she entered the main lobby, the security guard gave a nod to a guy sitting in a lobby chair, and Crystal began to walk towards the elevator.

Three men appeared in front of her, and the middle man said, "Miss Edwards?"

Before she could answer, Pete walked up to Crystal, took her hand and pulled her through the line of men. While doing so, Pete said to go to the elevator and don't look back, then turned to face his attackers.

One of the attackers said, "Hey, what do you think you're doing?"

Pete just smiled as the first attacker charged him. Pete hit the attacker in the jaw, sending him to the floor just as the second attacker swung. Pete ducked and hit him in the stomach, then the chin, making him fall down. When Pete turned, the third attacker had a knife, and he slashed Pete across his chest. Pete grabbed the attacker's arm that held the knife, then kicked the attackers knee. At the same time, snapping the attacker's wrist that held the knife. The attacker let out a scream and fell.

Pete looked at his shirt, and while walking to the lobby's front doors, said to himself, "Shit, my sister just gave me this shirt." Pete hailed a taxi, as he was getting in, he told the driver to take him to the Wolfinger Hotel, and he could hear the police sirens in the background.

Pete walked into his sister's waiting room, went up to the receptionist and said, "I need to see my sister immediately."

The receptionist looked up and saw the blood on Pete's shirt, and she replied, "Okay, please go to examination room three. I'll get your sister right away."

He replied, "Thank you."

Pete was looking at charts on the wall in the examination room while waiting for assistance when he heard the door open. He turned to see a pretty young nurse standing in the doorway.

He said, "Hi."

She replied, "Wow, you're big, muscular, and handsome."

Pete replied, "Thank you — two out of three isn't bad, but where is my sister?"

Just then, his sister Joanne came in, and when she saw that his new shirt was covered in blood she said, "What the hell did you do to your shirt? I just bought it for you, and you know your size is hard to find." As she walked over to him, she kissed him on the cheek, and said, "Take off your shirt, and let's see the damage."

Joanne turned to the young nurse, Donna, and said, "Get me butterflies, tape, and waterproof bandages." When Joanne finished, she said, "Try not to get in any more trouble. Your chest has a big X on it. While you are here let me see your back."

Pete turned and showed his sister. While she examined him, her eyes started to fill up with tears, and she said in a chokey voice, "The wounds are healing nicely. If you have a problem, come see me immediately."

Pete turned to see her crying and said, "I will." Then he hugged her and kissed her on her cheek, then kissed Donna as he walked out the back door.

Donna said to his sister, "I'm in love with him."

Joanne said, "You and every other woman. Now help me clean up."

Once in his apartment, Pete took a shower, put on clean clothes, and was just about to sit down and relax when the doorbell rang. He walked over to the door. When he opened it, he saw Crystal, some young lady, and his friend Joe standing there.

Pete said, "Please come in and sit down. To what do I owe this pleasure?"

Crystal replied, "Well, we just came to see how you are doing. This is my sister, Bernadette, and I thought we should all meet now that the three of us own the company."

Pete said, "I guess everything went well?"

Crystal said, "Yes, but tomorrow you have to go see Aunt Margaret and sign some papers."

Pete replied, "What time?"

Crystal replied, "About 10 o'clock."

Pete said, "That's great, because Joe and I have to go to medical, right Joe?"

Joe nodded, then said to Bernadette, "Are you single?"

She replied, "Yes."

Joe said, "Great, would you do me the pleasure of having dinner with me tomorrow night at 7 here at Josephine's?"

Bernadette said, "Yes, I would like that."

Joe said, "Great! It is a date. By the way, you two can come if you want."

Crystal got up and said, "I truly can't. I have to leave the country for about four to five weeks. I hope you understand."

Joe said, "No problem."

Joe and Bernadette then got up and said, "We are leaving."

Crystal said, "I will be right there," and she turned to Pete and said, "I don't like to mix business with pleasure, as you know, but I promise you when this business is done, you will have pleasure, and that you will not forget it." She kissed him and left.

The next day, Pete put on his uniform, met Joe downstairs, and went to the base to pick up their orders. It stated that they would be stationed in Fort Piece four days a week as instructors. The rest of the week they were to practice.

They then headed for the Edwards building. It was about 9:30 when the elevator doors opened. Pete and Joe were amazed by how many employees the Edwards company had, and most were surprisingly women. As Pete and Joe headed towards the receptionist, the women were looking at them, wondering what Pete and Joe were doing there.

When Pete and Joe reach the reception, Pete told her, "We are here to see Margaret Edwards."

The receptionist said, "She is waiting for you. Please take the aisle on the right and follow it to the end. Her office is on the right."

Pete thanked her.

When they reached the office, Pete was about to knock when they heard, "Please come in."

Once in the office, everybody introduced themselves, and then Margaret said, "Please sit down. My nieces speak very highly of both of you. It's very nice of you, Pete, to help her out and protect her. You will do well because she is a go-getter. It's also nice meeting you, Joseph, as Bernadette speaks highly of you. But they did not say you were in the military, especially special forces. My friend is in the Air Force. Maybe you know him — General Henry Jetson?"

Pete and Joe said, "No, we've never had the pleasure of meeting him."

Joe then said, "I'm in love with Bernadette and plan on marrying her."

Margaret and Pete both looked surprised.

Margaret replied, "If Bernadette should feel the same way, you will have to sign a prenuptial agreement."

Joe said, "Please let me have it now."

Margaret took out a piece of paper and gave it to Joe, saying, "You're sure of yourself."

Joe looked at the paper and crossed out the amount of money and put '$0', and then handed it back to Margaret, saying, "I do not want to be rewarded with money should I fail to keep my marriage."

Margaret put the paper away and said, "Let's get these papers signed so everyone can be on their way. Pete, you are now 1/3 owner of the company, but Crystal makes all the decisions."

Pete replied, "No problem. Just tell me where to sign."

Once all the papers were signed, Pete and Joe were about to leave when Margaret said, "Joe, Bernadette said you are taking her out to dinner. May I ask where?"

Joe replied, "Josephine's."

Margaret replied, "Of course. It's the best place in Florida. Maybe we'll see each other there, you never know."

As Pete and Joe were passing the receptionist, they heard on the intercom radio the song "Let's Dance" by Chris Magnus. Joe grabbed the inter-office mic and said, "All right everybody! This is the best song ever made, so let's dance! Stand in the aisle and as we come down, we will dance with you. Now let's start clapping your hands."

As the song played, Pete and Joe each took a side of the main aisle and started dancing with each girl standing in the aisle as they worked their way to the elevator. With perfect timing, the elevator door opened. When they reached it, Pete and Joe turned and bowed, and everyone was cheering and laughing when a voice came over the intercom, "Okay, let's get back to work."

About three weeks later, Pete's doorbell rang. When he opened the door, his friend Joe and Bernadette were standing there.

Joe said to Pete, "Congratulate us! We just got married."

Pete look stunned, but replied, "Congratulations to you both! Come in and sit down. I'll get a few beers and we will toast to your marriage."

After the toast, Joe said, "I wanted you to be the first to know."

Pete replied, "Thanks! Do Bernadette's parents know?"

Joe replied, "Not yet."

Pete said, "Where are you going to stay?"

Joe replied, "Between Bernadette and myself, we're flushed with cash. I'm going to ask your mother if we could lease a penthouse here. You don't have any problems with that, do you Pete?"

Pete replied, "Of course not! You are my best friend. It's strictly up to my parents. I would love to have you live here — not that we will see each other much since you are an old married man."

They both laughed.

Joe said, "Now we are off to tell her parents."

Pete wished them the best as they left.

Three Months Later

*P*ete was in his penthouse, sitting on the couch in his shorts when he heard the doorbell ring. Bear did not bark, so he knew it was a friend, and when he opened the door, Crystal was standing there.

She said, "Hello, handsome." She gave him a passionate kiss, then took his hand and started walking towards the bedroom while saying, "We're no longer partners. In this envelope is your share — 1/3 of what we got for selling the company."

As she lead him to the bedroom, she turned and said to Bear, "Go lie down . . . We are going to be busy for a while."

Once in his room, she shut the door, and started unzipping his pants. As his pants fell to the ground, she smiled. She started unzipping her dress, saying, "I see you missed me, too," and she gently pushed him back onto the bed.

As she got on top of him, Pete could feel her breasts lying on his chest, which aroused him even more. While kissing him, she took his manhood and slid it inside her, and the rest was a blur. When they were finished, they were both soaking wet. They stayed in bed the rest of the day, making love until the early evening.

Crystal said to Pete, "I'm hungry and in the mood for pizza."

Pete replied, "Well, the best pizza in Florida is made at NYPD Pizzeria, and my friend Gary owns it. What do you say we take a shower and then we'll go grab a bite?"

Crystal replied, "You shower first, then I will shower."

Pete said, "Why don't you want to shower together?"

Crystal said, "You know what will happen if we do, and I'm hungry."

As they left the pizzeria and walked toward Pete's car, Crystal stopped and said, "Pete, I have something to tell you."

Pete replied, "What?"

Crystal said, "I think you're very handsome, very lovable, and I really thought that if you would love me, I would stay. But I know you don't love me, so I'm going back to Hong Kong. I enjoyed being with you, and I hope someday that you will find someone. Besides, one special forces military man in the family is enough."

She smiled as she gave him a passionate kiss. Just then, a taxi pulled up, and Pete was surprised.

Crystal said, "I called when I went to the ladies' room. Remember when you open up the envelope, we would've had nothing if you hadn't come to my aid. For that, I will always be grateful."

She blew him a kiss, got into the taxi and left.

Pete stood there for a moment, then said to himself, "I wonder if I will ever understand women." He then got in his car and headed home.

Once home, he took Bear for a walk, and then headed back to the penthouse. He sat at the table looking at the envelope for a few moments, wondering what she had meant by finding true love. He opened the envelope and found a letter in with the check. It read:

I love you, and without your support, this sale would have never happened. Yes, it's $30 million. We sold the company for $90 million and we would not have even gotten that if it weren't for your support. I will always think of you and love you. Part of the deal was for me to be the CEO in Hong Kong for two years, which I have no objection to. Wishing you the best and hope you find true love.

Love, Crystal

Pete looked at the check and said, "Wow, our tax accountant is going to have her hands full this year."

The next morning, Pete went to the bank located in the hotel. The young teller was afraid to deposit such a large check, so she called over the manager. The manager looked at the check and gave his approval.

Pete asked, "How long before it clears?"

The manager replied, "About a week, Mr. Wolfinger."

Pete said, "Thank you," and left.

About two weeks later, at the family dinner, Pete said, "Before we start, you will see an envelope in front of you. This is a gift from me to you. I invested in a company and became an one-third owner, where Crystal and Bernadette were my partners. Crystal then sold the company for $90 million, my share being thirty million. I want to give each couple $5 million. You only have to pay the taxes."

Everyone got up, went to Pete, and thanked him.

Pete said, "I'm glad everyone is happy. Now let's eat! I am starving."

The Request

The days turned into weeks and the weeks turned into months. One evening, Pete got a call from Margaret asking him to meet her at Josephine's for a drink at 7 o'clock the next day.

Pete replied, "Okay, I'll be there."

When Pete arrived, Margaret and the general were sitting at the table with drinks. Margaret asked Pete to sit down and offered him a drink.

Pete replied, "I'll have a Jack and ginger."

After his drink arrived, Margaret said, "Pete, I'd like to ask you a big favor. But before I do, I'd like to tell you a story."

Pete replied, "Okay, I'm listening."

Margaret said, "When I was a young girl, I was sent from Ireland to England to study business law. I went under my mother's maiden name, Ebert, because my family is very wealthy. As you know, they own one of the largest import-export businesses. While I was studying, I fell in love with a man ten years older than me, and when I graduated, I did not return home but stayed with him. This made my family very angry, but we were in love. Then after a year, he came home one day and said he must leave and that I should forget him.

"A few months after he left, I found out that I was pregnant, and I did not know what to do. I was really scared. I called my parents, and they were mad, but forgave me. They came to England to help me set up another import-export business from London. They told me that I should stay in London while my brother and his wife would be in charge of the Florida branch. My parents told my brother that my husband was killed in a car accident while I was carrying Judy. My brother and I were never close as he is about seven years older than me. I'm not sure if Bernadette and Crystal are aware that they even have a cousin.

"Then, about a month ago, I read that King Philip of Lampicki was ill, and had about six months to live. The paper showed a picture of him, and I realized that he was my lover, but I had only ever known him as Kevin. Then I read that everyone in line for the throne was being assassinated. The killers somehow know where to find them all."

Margaret and the general then told him the plan, and after finishing, Margaret said, "Are you okay with this?"

Pete replied, "Yes, but I have some questions."

Margaret said, "Shoot."

Pete asked, "1. Does Judy have any boyfriends — old or new?"

Margaret said that she had no boyfriend and kept mainly to her studies.

"2. Is Judy aware of the situation?"

Margaret replied, "Yes, I informed her over the phone, and she said she would be willing to go along with the plan."

"3. Why are you here in America?"

Margaret replied, "My brother's wife is very sick and he asked for me to come and help him."

"4. What do I tell my family?"

Margaret replied, "Tell them that you met online and fell in love. But remember that she is a virgin, and she should stay that way until she is really married. Don't get any ideas — your marriage is fake."

"5. What do I do for my job?"

She stated, "The general said that as of today that you only report to me. Tell no one of your assignment, including Joe. I will take care of all records and pay."

"6. When do I leave?"

The general replied, "Margaret will leave tonight on her company jet, and you will leave tomorrow at 8 p.m. You are to report to Fort Piece, a colonial. Higgins will fly you by fighter jet to our military base in London. Wear only civilian clothes and bring only your wallet and ID. When you arrive, Sergeant Di Janic will be waiting for you. He will take you to a room where you will be given your uniform, passports for you and your wife, the address for where to go, and £400. You should arrive in London around 1 a.m. Any questions?"

Pete replied, "No, sir."

Pete returned to his penthouse, called Joe, and asked if he would take care of Bear for a few days.

"And please call Joseph from Abstract Plumbing to fix the kitchen faucet. When I come back, I will tell you what is happening."

London

*T*he jet landed in London around 1 a.m., and Sergeant Di Janic was there waiting for Pete. Sergeant Di Janic informed Pete that his uniform was not ready and that it wouldn't be for a few hours.

It was 5:30 in the evening when Pete knocked on Margaret's apartment door.

Margaret opened the door. When she saw Pete, she looked surprised, saying, "I thought you had changed your mind."

Pete replied, "No, I would never do that. Just had a few setbacks. I have our passports, plane tickets, and Judy's Florida driver's license."

Margaret said, "Great. Come in and wait here. Judy will be out in a few moments. I must go get the reverend." She shut the door behind her.

Pete looked around, thinking it was a very nice one-bedroom apartment. It had a kitchen, dining area, and a living room that overlooked the city. Then Pete spotted a picture on the wall. He walked over to look at it and saw that it was Margaret and the general when they were very young.

Just then, he heard a feminine voice say, "Hello," and he turned towards the voice, seeing a young woman. No words could describe her beauty.

Stunned, Pete could not respond.

She said, "My name is Judy. You must be my bodyguard."

Pete replied, "Yes."

Judy said, "I'm surprised my mother would allow a strong and handsome man like you to be my bodyguard."

Pete blushed and thanked her for the compliment.

Just then, Judy's mother, Margaret, came in with the deacon and his wife, Lori.

Margaret said, "I see you two have now met. This is Deacon Tony Giorgio and his wife, Lori, from *Living With Victory Ministries*. He will perform the marriage and Lori will be the witness."

The deacon said, "Before we begin, do you have the rings?"

Margaret stepped forward and handed him a wedding ring while saying, "This is for my daughter."

Judy said, "Where is his wedding ring?"

Margaret said, "He doesn't get one."

Judy replied, "That's not right. I'll be right back."

She went into the bedroom and came out with a bunch of hoop earrings. She tried each one on his ring finger until she found one that fit. Then she looked up at Pete and said, "Now we both have rings."

Pete smiled and thanked her.

After the ceremony, Judy, Pete, and Lori signed the marriage license, and once it was completed, Margaret said, "If the marriage is not consummated, can she get an annulment?"

Tony said, "That is correct."

Margaret said, "Great, thank you," as she escorted them to the door. "Okay, let's get ready for bed. Judy and I are going to sleep in the bedroom. You can sleep on the big easy chair. When we are done using the bathroom, I'll tell you, and then you can use the bathroom."

Pete replied, "Okay." He then went over to the big easy chair, sat down, and started looking at an old magazine as he waited for the ladies to get done.

It was around 11 p.m. when Pete heard Margaret say, "You may now use the bathroom. I left clean towels, soap, and a razor for you. Goodnight — see you at 7 a.m. tomorrow."

Pete replied, "Thank you." He waited for two to three hours before using the bathroom. After washing up, Pete started to shave, but the mirror kept fogging up, so he left the bathroom door open. He'd just finished when he looked up and saw Margaret in the mirror standing there with a glass in her hand.

She said, "I'm sorry, I came for a glass of water and the door was open. I assumed the bathroom was empty."

Pete said, "No problem," as he took the glass and started the cold water running in the sink.

Margaret said, "So many scars on what looks like a perfect body. It looks like you were used for target practice. Why stay a soldier?"

Pete gave the glass of water to Margaret and said, "Someone must keep freedom free."

Margaret thanked him for the water and started for the door. Then she turned with tears in her eyes, saying, "Thank you for my freedom," and then turned and entered the bedroom.

It was about 7 a.m., and Pete was sitting at the kitchen table fully dressed.

When Margaret came out of the bedroom, she said to Pete, "I'm leaving. Please remember your promise. Judy is a virgin and she should stay that way until she finds the man she loves."

Pete replied, "Yes, I understand."

Margaret replied, "Good," and left.

Judy came out about 20 minutes later, looking beautiful. Smiling, she said, "I'm sorry I took so long. I'm ready for my new adventure."

Once in the taxi, Pete told the driver to go to the London airport, and that if there is a jewelry store on the way, please stop.

Judy looked at Pete, and Pete said, "It is a surprise."

About 10 minutes later, the driver pulled up in front of a jewelry store and turned towards Pete, saying, "I know this jewelry store, and the owner is a fair person."

While getting out, Pete said, "Thank you, please wait here." When Pete and Judy got to the front door, the jeweler buzzed them in, and Pete asked to see wedding bands and engagement rings.

Judy said, "I have a wedding band."

Pete said, "You need one to match your beauty."

The jeweler showed Judy a few different ones, and Judy picked out the rings she liked, asking Pete, "Can we afford this?"

Pete replied, "Yes," while he gave his platinum American Express card to the jeweler.

The jeweler said, "The total is going to be —" but before he could finish, Pete interrupted.

"We don't want to know."

The jeweler ran the card. The phone rang immediately, and the jeweler picked it up, handing it to Pete, saying, "It's American Express."

Pete took the phone, saying, "Yes, I approve this purchase. Thank you." Then he gave the phone back to the jeweler.

While admiring her rings, Judy looked at Pete, hugged him, and kissed him on the lips. While smiling, she said, "When you divorce me, you are not getting them back."

And Pete said, "May that day never come," and they were both quiet for a few seconds. Then Pete took her hand, and headed for the door. As they were heading towards the taxi, Pete noticed three or four young men hanging out on the corner, looking towards him and Judy. The taxi driver got out with a baseball bat and stood by the door. Pete quickly put Judy in the taxi and turned to see one young man jogging towards him. Pete was ready to fight, but the man stopped short and put out his hand.

He said, "Thank you for your service. Hank, my brother, served over there too, and I'm going to be going there next year."

Pete replied, "You're welcome. Be safe and keep your head down," as he got into the taxi.

The driver then got in the car and put his bat back under the seat, heading for the airport.

Judy and Pete got out of the taxi while the driver got the luggage, and Pete took all the English currency and gave the money to the driver.

The driver said, "That is way too much."

Pete replied, "Not for a man who was willing to back up a stranger." Pete took the luggage and Judy's hand and headed for the gate. They'd just made it when the announcement came over the intercom saying that first class passengers may board. Pete gave the flight attendant the tickets.

She said to take any seat. "You're the only ones flying first class."

Pete asked, "Where do you want to sit?"

Judy replied, "By the window."

Pete just smiled as he sat down.

Some time later, Judy said, "Excuse me, I have to use the ladies' room."

Pete said, "Sure," as he got up for her to pass.

A few minutes later, as Judy was returning to her seat, she heard the two stewardesses talking and looking at Pete. She heard them say, "If he were mine, I would use and abuse him."

As Judy passed, she said to the same stewardesses, "I plan on it."

They all laughed, and when she got to her seat, Pete asked, "What was all the laughing about?"

As she sat down, she smiled, and said, "Maybe, just maybe, someday I'll let you know."

The plane landed, they got their luggage, and caught a taxi. They did not arrive at the hotel until 5:30 p.m. When they got out of the taxi, Pete asked Tim, the bellboy, to bring the luggage up to the penthouse. While Judy was admiring the hotel, Pete gave Tim the earring with instructions to give it to the jeweler. "Turn it into a ring size thirteen without destroying the shape of the earring," he said. Then, he turned to Judy and said, "Ready to meet the family?"

Judy smiled and said, "Yes."

When they entered the dining room, everyone stood up and congratulated them while introducing themselves, asking to see the rings.

Judy looked at Pete and smiled.

After a while Mr. W said, "Let's all sit down before the food gets cold."

Everyone was excited and continued to talk. Judy fell in love with his family. They made her feel like she was part of the family, and after dinner, everyone started to return to what they were doing before dinner.

Before leaving, Joe told Pete, "Bear is in the penthouse."

Pete thanked him.

Pete's mom said that she is having a party Friday night for Judy and him in the restaurant, and that it will start at 6. "Don't be late."

While in the elevator, Judy looked up at Pete, smiling and said, "Do you believe in love at first sight?"

Pete smiled back and said, "Yes, I do. And I believe this is one of those times."

She hugged him, and said, "I think so too."

Just then, the elevator doors opened up, they walked into the foyer. Pete said, "Are you afraid of dogs?"

Judy replied, "No, I love dogs — even big ones."

Pete said, "Great, because Bear is very big." Pete opened the door, and they saw Bear sitting there, his tail was wagging back-

and forth. Pete got down on his knees and hugged him while saying, "This is Judy. You will be guarding her — understand?"

Bear looked up at Judy and barked.

She got down on her knees and kissed him all over his face.

Bear's tail started wagging faster.

Pete said, "That is it! Love at first sight."

While showing Judy the layout of the penthouse, Pete stopped in the library and saw a FedEx package on his desk. He took it and handed to Judy while saying, "This is for you."

Judy said, "Thank you. Should I open it?"

Pete replied, "Yes."

Judy opened the box and saw a stainless steel Platinum American Express card. Judy said, "Pete, can you really afford something like this?"

Pete said, "Before I answer, please open the checkbook."

Judy opened the checkbook, seeing a balance of $17 million. Judy stood there staring at the book. She looked up at Pete and said, "I have so many questions."

Pete laughed, saying, "It is a long story, but this is our money."

Judy hugged him and said, "Then we will have to invest."

Pete replied, "No problem. It's all yours to do with whatever you want. Now please let me escort you to the master bedroom, which is across from mine. You should have everything you need. If not, call room service. Bear will be by your side at all times."

Judy gave Pete a quick kiss and thanked him as she slid the bedroom door closed.

Pete walked to his bedroom, while saying to himself, "I have a dilemma."

The next day Pete got up at the usual time, 4:45 a.m., did his routine calisthenics, took a shower, had breakfast, and sat down to read his paper. He heard Judy moving around in the bedroom, so he knew she was up.

The doorbell rang, and he looked at his watch. It was 9 a.m. He was wondering who that could be when he opened the door and Candy grabbed him, giving him a big kiss.

Her husband was behind her and said, "Hey, Candy!"

Candy said, "Just want him to know what he is missing and what you have. Now, where is the woman who stole your heart?"

Pete said, "In the master bedroom."

Candy headed that way, and Pete said, "Come on in, James. Want a beer? How are the kids?"

James replied, "Yes to the beer, and the kids are great."

Just when Pete and James had sat down on the couches, they heard Judy yell, "I can't believe it's Candy, right here in my bedroom!"

Then they heard laughing, and Candy yelled, "Pete, she is beautiful."

Then everything went quiet. James and Pete looked at each other and started laughing. They were still laughing when Candy and Judy came out of the bedroom and headed for the front door. Candy said, "Enjoy your day, boys. Go play golf. Judy and I are going shopping."

James and Pete looked at each other, and James said, "That sounds great to me. What do you say? Nine holes or eighteen?"

Pete said, "Let's try eighteen. We could always stop."

It was 5:30 when the family sat down as usual to have dinner. Judy and Candy were not back from shopping yet.

James said they had to leave tomorrow. Candy had a show and his mother was watching the kids, so he wanted to get back as soon as possible.

Everybody said they were sorry to hear that and they hoped they return soon.

Jim said, "Of course we will. Candy thinks of you as her family."

Mr. W replied, "We certainly think of her as our daughter."

Pete was working out in his gym when he heard the front door open. He looked at his watch, and it was 8 p.m. He put his robe on and then went to the front door.

Judy was standing there smiling. She thanked Tim, the bellhop, for bringing up all her things.

Tim said, "No problem," as he shut the door.

Judy walked over to Pete and said, "I had the most amazing day! I still cannot believe I shopped all day with the famous Candy." She then hugged Pete and kissed him.

Pete stepped back and said, "You should go shopping more often."

Judy started crying.

Pete said, "Did I say the wrong thing?"

Judy said, "No, it's just that I'm your wife, and I've never seen your scars. My mother has seen them and Candy has seen them, but I have not. And when Candy asked me, I did not know what to say, so I told the truth. I don't notice them because I love you, and I only see you."

Pete hugged her, then took off his robe, showing all his scars.

Judy started crying saying, "There are so many."

Pete said, "I will show you a scar no one has seen." He turned around, pulled his shorts down, and showed her a scar on the left cheek of his butt. While he pulled up his shorts, he turned and kissed her. He whispered her ear, "Now you have seen more than them. Now let's go see what you bought."

Pete sat in Judy's bedroom and watched, smiling, as Judy opened the packages she had bought. Judy was smiling and laughing as she did so. She said, "You can't see some of them because they're unmentionables."

After opening all the packages, there was one left hanging on the luggage rack, and Pete said, "What about that one?"

She smiled, saying, "That's for tomorrow night when we go to dinner. I want to surprise you."

It was Friday, and everyone was excited about the dinner for Judy and Pete.

Judy got up early and left about 10 a.m. with Bear, saying to Pete that she would be home at about 3 p.m., and not to worry because she had her phone and Bear with her.

After she left, Pete tracked her phone to the beauty parlor downstairs. It made him feel better knowing that she was close by. He checked in with the general, who said there was no news about the king. Unknowns' group was still looking to kill anyone with blood ties to the king.

At about 3:30, Judy came in with a kerchief around her, threw Pete a kiss, and ran into her bedroom.

It was 5:45 p.m., and Pete and Bear waited outside Judy's bedroom. They were both dressed in their formal uniforms.

Judy came out of the bedroom, and her beauty took Pete's breath away. He could not believe that the Lord had made such a beautiful woman, and that she loved him. Her hair was platinum blonde, and she wore a formfitting blue sequined gown that showed off her perfect body and a sapphire necklace with matching earrings.

She moved closer to him and kissed him on the cheek, saying, "Do you like my dress?"

Pete replied, "You're beautiful."

She said, "Thank you. The necklace and earrings were a gift from Candy. She said that something blue should be worn, so she bought me this to match my blue sequin dress." With love in her eyes, she said, "I want you to be proud of me."

Pete replied, "No matter what you wear or do, I will be proud of you because I love you."

While going down in the elevator, Judy said, "Candy will have a camera man there. She wants pictures."

Pete smiled and said, "So will I."

They walked across the main lobby to Josephine's, and people stopped to look and admire the couple. Once inside Josephine's, every eye was on them as they walked to the family table. After everyone introduced themselves, they all sat down for dinner.

Charlie made his famous goulash, Connie made a cake that had a soldier and bride on top, and everyone was having a great time.

Then Margaret said to Judy, "I heard you could sing. Why don't you sing us a song?"

As she glared at her mother, everyone said, "Please?"

Judy finally said, "Okay, but only one."

When she walked to the staged with Pete, everyone watched. Once on stage, she told the three-piece band what to play, and she walked over to the mic. She told the audience, "This song is for my husband, and it is called *Will You Love Me Tomorrow?*"

The whole audience went quiet, you couldn't hear a pin drop.

When she finished, everyone stood up and yelled for more.

She said, "Okay, one more, but that is it! This song is also for my husband. It is called *Everywhere.*"

The audience went silent again.

After Judy finished, the audience stood up and cheered, clapping as Judy walked offstage.

When they returned to the table, Judy smiled and said, "We are calling it a night."

As Judy and Pete walked out, every eye was on them.

Once in the penthouse, Pete walked Judy to her bedroom.

She kissed him, saying, "Goodnight," and then she shut her bedroom door.

Pete walked into his bedroom, saying to himself, "I don't think anybody could understand women." He took off his uniform, and then laid on the bed, looking at the moonlight shining on the ocean before slowly falling asleep.

Sometime later he woke to the sound of Judy's voice. When he looked at the foot of his bed, he saw her standing there as she let her robe fall, standing like the Venus of Love statue. Pete quickly went to her. She put her hands up and stopped him from coming any closer.

She said, "Pete, I have one gift that I can give to the man I love. I can never give it again, nor can I ever get it back. Tonight I want to give it to you, for you are the man I love."

She gently reached out to him and pulled him close to her while giving him a passionate kiss. Pete picked her up and laid her on his bed. As he laid down beside her, he felt her nervousness, and he gently kissed her while slowly moving his hand down to her womanhood. She stopped his hand but then released it. He gently massaged her womanhood, and when he felt that she was moist, he got on top of her while whispering in her ear, "You can stop me anytime you want. I love you."

He slowly entered her womanhood. She got tense, but then she relaxed after he entered.

She grabbed his butt cheeks while whispering in his ear, "Faster!"

And after a few moments, they both climaxed together, then laid there together in bed, each other professing their undying love for the other.

The next morning, after making love and taking a shower, they got dressed. They ordered room service.

As they sat down at the kitchen table, Judy started to cry.

Pete gently grabbed her hand, asking what the problem was.

Judy said, "I love it here. I love everything here. I don't want to leave, and I don't want to leave you."

Pete said, "I have a duty to fulfill. I promise you I will never leave you — ever."

She smiled.

A few weeks passed, and Judy and Pete were in bed sleeping. At about 2 o'clock in the morning, Pete's phone rang. He picked it up and said, "Hello?"

General Jetson said, "You've got about fifteen minutes to get ready. Judy's been compromised. Three assassins are heading your way."

Then the phone went silent.

Pete jumped out of bed, put on his pants, checked his weapons, and put on his weapons belt. While running into the bathroom, he grabbed a sleeping pill, which he'd had from when he first came home, and a glass of water. He ran over to Judy, woke her up, and said, "Judy, please take this."

Half asleep, she said, "What is wrong?"

Pete said nothing as he picked her up in his arms and carried her to the secret room. He grabbed a lounging blanket on the way, and by the time they got to the secret room, Judy was sleeping. Pete gently laid her in the chair and said to Bear, "Protect — do not bark." Then Pete shut the door.

He was just coming out of the library when he heard the lock on the front door turn. Pete said to himself, "Shit, I thought that it would take a little more time to open than that."

Two assassins came in wearing night vision glasses. They turned to the right and headed towards the master bedrooms. Pete considered it foolish of them to pass the other rooms without checking. Pete quietly came out and shot one assassin in the back of the head. The other turned, and before he could fire, Pete shot him in the throat. Pete walked over to the bodies, checking to make sure both were dead. The assassin that was shot in the throat was still breathing, so Pete took a pillow from the couch and smothered him until he stopped breathing. He took their weapons and put them in the library desk draw. Pete ran down the fire exit steps to the garage, slowly opening the door. He saw a white van with an assassin who was outside of the truck, smoking a cigar and holding a gun. He was talking to a person next to him who had his hands tied.

The assassin heard a noise, and he looked up. As soon as he saw Pete, he lifted his gun to shoot, but Pete shot first, killing the assassin instantly.

The man with his hands tied started to scream, "Please don't shoot! Please don't shoot! I have no gun!"

Pete said, "Don't move," as he walked over and checked the body. Pete picked up the assassin's gun and put it in his pocket. He then turned to the person with his hand tied and said, "Explain, or you will be lying next to him."

The person said, "My name is Ken Taylor. I know the Edwards family."

Pete put the gun to the man's head, saying, "Talk or I will kill you now."

Ken started to cry. "Okay, I will! I went to Mrs. Margaret Edwards to ask for a loan. I was about to enter her office when I heard her talking on her phone to her daughter. She was saying, 'Judy, I know you love Pete, but you're my daughter and the soon-to-be queen of Lampicki.' When she saw me, she quickly hung up the phone and asked what I wanted. I told her I needed a loan, and she said, 'No — go away!'

"I went home and started searching on the dark web, hoping to find fast money. Then I came across a bulletin that said: 'Large reward to anyone who can prove blood relation to the king of Lampicki. Please contact this number.' So I did, and the next night these guys come to my door, put a bag of money on the table, tied my hands, and said, 'Show us where this Judy is!' And here we are."

Pete said, "What were the names of the people who contacted you?"

Ken said, "They never gave me a name, but the guy you shot said they were the prime minster of Lampicki and the captain of the king's guard."

All this time, Pete's phone was on, so the general could hear.

Pete said, "General, what do you want to do?"

The general said, "Do what you want with him. The cleaners are on the way. I will take care of the other two." He then hung up.

Pete looked at Ken, who wet himself and started crying. "Please don't kill me!"

Pete said, "I want you to take this van back to your place and get what you need. Go on the dark web, tell them she was killed and the assassins were killed in a gun fight. No one noticed you so you were able to get out. Then destroy the computer and your phone. Take the van and drive to a Walmart. Leave the van there, and then run and never come back. Do you understand?"

He nodded his head, jumped in the van and took off, just as the cleaners showed up. They cleaned the garage first and then went up with Pete to the penthouse. They were fast and excellent. After they left, Pete went into the secret room, and Judy was still sleeping. He gently picked her up and put her in bed, then took a shower and went to bed himself.

The next morning, Pete got up with very little sleep, walked Bear, did his exercises, practiced his karaka, took another shower, and then woke Judy up while gently kissing her. "Good morning, my Queen. Breakfast is being ordered."

"Good morning, my King. Thank you. I will be out in a few minutes," replied Judy.

When Judy went to sit down, she said, "Something is different." As she looked around, she said, "My blanket and the pillow from the couch are missing."

"Bear destroyed the pillow while playing with it, and the maid took the blanket to clean."

Judy looked at Bear and said, "I don't care. I love you." She kissed and hugged him. Just then Judy's phone rang. She said, "Hello mother . . ." And then she said, "I don't care if he died, I don't want to be queen . . . I don't care that you had our marriage cancelled . . . Okay, I will go, but Pete, Bear, Joe, and Bernadette go, too . . . If the air field is only good for very small planes then get two planes. When do we leave? . . . Tomorrow, at 11:00? I will tell everyone."

She hung up the phone, then ran to Pete. She put her arms around him and started crying. Pete gently stroked her hair while saying that everything would work out.

Sometime later, Pete held an emergency family meeting. Once all were there, Judy and Pete told them about her becoming queen. They all hugged her while saying that they would miss her, Joe, and Bernadette, and that they couldn't come now, but would the first chance they can.

The next day, everyone was out in front of the hotel waving so long as Judy and Pete got into the limo. Once in, the limo headed for the airport. Margaret and the general were in the limo already.

Margaret said, "We are going to meet the advisor to the king. The prime minister and the captain of the guard were killed in an accident."

Once at the airport, the luggage was loaded along with a lie detector box. Pete said, "Great, we will use this on the rest of the palace guards."

Even in a luxury jet, it was a long trip.

The pilot said, "Please put your seat belts on. This is not a real air strip. It has torches for lights."

Once the plane landed, two old limos pulled up, and a gentleman asked them to please get in the car. "The others will get your luggage."

They rode for about an hour and then pulled up to what looked like a building out of *Downton Abbey*. The driver said with pride, "This is the palace of Lampicki."

Once the cars stopped, a valet came out, opened the doors, and asked for them to follow him. They were led to a large room, then asked to sit and wait. "The advisor will be with you shortly. Please ask the maid for anything you want."

After a few moments, a tall man and a beautiful woman walked through the door and introduced themselves as Igor and Roseanna Wisniewska, advisors to the former king and, hopefully, to the future queen.

After everyone introduced themselves, Igor said, "Please, let us show you to your rooms. We realize you've had a long day and must be tired. My wife, Roseanna, will show Mrs. Edwards and the general to their rooms. I will show the future queen and her bodyguard to their rooms. Tomorrow, we will have the coronation ceremony, formally making Judy the queen. I have made all the arrangements. It will start at 10 a.m. We have a TV and radio station coming to cover the event. The cardinal will do the ceremony. Now, let's get a good night's sleep."

Once in Judy's bedroom, Judy said to Igor, "I would like you to know that the captain and I were once married."

Igor smiled, saying, "I know. I could see the white band on your
fingers." As he walked over to the wall, he said, "For now, make
sure your doors are locked. Also, touch this spot here, and a door
will open to the captain's room, which is adjacent to yours." As
Igor was leaving the room, he said, "Please wear gloves tomorrow. Goodnight."

The next day, wearing her grandmother's gown, Judy was
crowned Queen of Lampicki. As she stood on the balcony waving, the people cheered. The radio and TV announcers said, "I
believe we have the prettiest queen. And let's not to leave out her
very handsome bodyguard and guard dog that looks like a lion."

That night, Igor and Roseanna told the family, "Tomorrow will
be the Queen's Ball. Judy can wear her grandmother's gown."

Igor said, "The ball is held so that other royals get to meet you,
and you can meet them."

The Queen's Ball

*M*argaret and the general watched from the balcony as the guests started to arrive early, at about 5:30 p.m. Igor and Roseanna noticed that there were no cancellations, and at precisely 6 p.m., Judy started down the stairway.

The people stopped talking, they looked up, and there were whispers about how beautiful the queen looked as she walked down the stairs. When she reached the bottom, Igor walked over and took her hand. He signaled for the band to start, and the captain walked over to Roseanna and asked her to dance.

After a while, the guests joined in, and at the end of the dance, Judy went and stood in the center of Igor and Roseanna. The men started to line up to get a chance to dance with her, and she danced all night, never getting a break. She got proposals from princes and kings, but her heart was only for the captain. She was getting jealous watching the women standing by him, but his heart belonged to the queen and his eyes were always on her.

Towards the end of the evening, a young prince approached the captain. Looking like he'd had a few too many, the prince said, "Captain, you should not look at the queen like that." Then he started to swing at the captain.

But the captain caught the prince's hand and gave him a light shot to the throat. The prince begin to choke, and the captain said loudly, "He is okay. I will take him out for some air."

Once outside, the captain fixed the prince so he could breathe, while saying, "I'm sorry, but you were going to cause a scene. I always watch the queen because that is my job. If you noticed, I cannot watch everyone that dances with my queen, but I can watch as they come close to her. Now, look at the dog, Bear. watch how his head moves. We are always on alert. Once they attempted to kill the queen, so we must always be alert."

The prince apologized, and while walking back to the ballroom, the prince smiled and said, "Thank you. And should you ever need a job, please come to me."

Pete replied, "Will do."

The rest of the evening went well.

The next day, Roseanna told the queen she has had 13 proposals. Then she turned to the captain and said, "Not to leave you out — you have five!"

Everyone just smiled.

Igor said, "Roseanna can show the queen the proposals and ledgers. I will show the captain the palace guards."

The queen agreed, saying, "But all of the captain's proposals must be thrown out!"

Everyone laughed and went their separate ways.

That morning after breakfast, the queen went to her office with Bear.

While the captain checked the palace guards, he set a table with a box on it. The captain said to the palace guards, "This is a lie detector. Every palace guard will be asked two questions. Firstly, are you loyal to the queen? Secondly, would you die for your queen? If you fail, you are dismissed from service. There are 130 of you, and I expect all to pass."

After the test, 128 palace guards had passed. The captain stood in front of the 128 men, saying, "You are going to take a physical exam. Those who pass will then do the physical calisthenics that I will show you. Should you fail, you will have two weeks in which to try again."

Two failed.

As Judy and Pete laid in bed, Judy said, "I'm worried. We went over the ledgers and found that the Bratva, the Russian mafia, has their hands in everything! They take a percent of the taxes we collect, they sell drugs, and they take our people and sell them. Not to mention they use a protection insurance against the store owners. We have no army and very few police, and they have about 200 members. They even have a castle by the low river as headquarters. Our country is 2,000 miles by 500 miles. We are connected to Russia from the north and west. To the south is the Pelka River, which is very shallow and leads to the Barenta Sea. To the east are mountains. We have a population of 150,000 citizens, and 85 percent of them are Russian. Our main source of income is grain, which we sell to Russia. I don't know where to start."

Pete said, "For now, let's get some sleep and talk about it tomorrow."

The next day, Judy woke up early. Smiling, she turned to Pete who was already up doing push-ups, and said, "Pete, go back to your room, unmake your bed, and take a shower."

As Pete was going to his room, he said, "Spoken like a true queen."

Judy threw the pillow at him, laughing.

While having breakfast, Judy said to everyone, "I would like to go to the TV and radio station."

Once at the station. Judy waited to go on air. Once on air, she said, "Citizens of Lampicki, I decree the following. Starting now, taxes will be 1 percent. Marijuana is legal. All citizens can carry guns, but they must be registered with the police. Prostitution will be made legal, of course with certain rules. There will be no more tax collectors — we will send our guards to your town to collect."

The Bratva leader was listening to the broadcast, and he was furious. He told his lieutenant, "Take 10 men and go to the TV and radio station. When the queen comes out, kill them. Use our signature knives — no guns. Remember to carve a 'B' in their bodies."

In the meantime, a reporter and camara man were hiding behind bushes waiting for the queen to come out of the station to take some candid pictures of her. And the citizens of Lampicki could not get enough news about the captain and the dog.

A short time later, the queen, captain, and Bear came out. The queen said to the captain, "I told the guard to bring the car up front, as it is such a beautiful day."

As they walked away from the entrance, a large black van pulled up and ten assassins came out of the truck with knives. They started to run towards the queen.

Pete put the queen behind him and threw four throwing stars at the attackers, killing all four. The remaining six attackers tried to get behind the captain to get to the queen, but that was not happening. Bear's size and growl kept the attackers from charging the queen. The captain was a blur as he kicked and hit the remaining attackers. Every time he hit an attacker, you could hear bones crack.

There were two remaining attackers, and one got past the captain, but the captain had one throw star left to throw. He knew it would leave his mid-section open to the last attacker, but he threw the star killing the attacker that was about to kill the queen.

The last attacker slashed the captain across mid-section, but the captain grabbed the attackers hand, breaking it while hitting him with a throat kill.

The captain turned towards the queen, telling her to run. And Bear protected the queen as the captain started to fall.

The queen started running up the steps, and she turned to see the captain on the ground. She stopped, turned, and ran to him. She sat down and put his head in her arms, crying, "Please don't die! You promised you would never leave me alone!"

She kept kissing him, and he slowly lifted his bloodied hand and put it to her cheek. She took it and kissed it, getting blood all over her face.

Just then, the guards and doctors arrived.

The reporter recorded all of this and turned the video in to the TV station. The video went viral.

The Lampicki citizens began attacking the Bratva, killing them. The Bratva were so scared that they ran to the Bratva headquarters. The boss said, "Not to worry. We have all the guns we need. They will never get inside this castle."

In the meantime, Margaret saw what just happened on TV. She said to the general, "Give me the number of that mercenary."

She went to the phone and called, and she said, "Hello, is this Daniel Pace, CEO of the I&A company? . . . Good, just the gentleman I was looking for. I'd like to hire your services . . . Yes, I know what you do, and I'm told by General Jetson that you do it well . . . Yes, I know you're expensive . . . Well, I want you to eliminate the Bratva that are holing up in a castle at low point in Lampicki . . . Yes, I can hold . . . Great! How fast and how much? I want them all dead . . . Oh, you are fighting in Ukraine now? . . . Okay, how much? . . . $8 million? Okay. $4 million now, and the other $4 million when you are done. When will you do your job? . . . In four hours? Great." Then she hung up.

The last words of the Bratva boss were: "No one can touch us."

Then, twelve rockets hit the castle, turning it to rubble. Five Black Hawk helicopters came out of the sky, making a circle. They fired machine guns into the rubble, then landed to check for anyone alive.

Mr. Pace called Margaret and said, "Done. No one is alive."

Margaret deposited the rest of the money, then turned to the general and said, "She is safe for now. Let's go to the hospital."

When they reached the hospital, Judy was in the waiting room, and Roseanna was trying to wash the blood off of her.

Judy was still in shock, and she turned and said to her mother, "He promised he wouldn't leave me!"

Margaret said, "He won't. He's young and strong."

Judy started crying while saying, "We will get married as soon as we can!"

And to her surprise, her mother said, "Yes, you will."

Just then, the doctor came out, walked over to the queen, and said, "Your captain will make it. He's in critical but stable condition since he lost a lot of blood. But I assure you that he will survive."

The relief on everybody's face was worth its weight in gold.

Three months later, the queen and the captain stood before the cardinal getting married. Joe and Bernadette and the rest of the family were there, and it was a joyous occasion.

The news of the wedding traveled all over the world, and the country of Lampicki was being noticed. Companies from all over the world were now looking at Lampicki to see if they could invest in the country.

Russia

A few weeks later, the Russian ambassador showed up at the palace and requested an emergency meeting with the queen. Igor came out to meet him, but the ambassador said, "I must speak to the queen."

As the ambassador stood before the queen, he said, "Before I say what I must, please let me show you the treaty your country and my country have. Your country was established in the year 1500 with the permission of our king, and your country has always been part of Russia. We have allowed you to exist because your little country could do no harm to us. But now you can, and therefore, according to the treaty, you must step down and Lampicki will once again become part of Russia.

"We will allow Lampicki to become a Russian state, and Igor will be prime minister. Your mother may keep the importing business. You may take four items from your palace, but the rest will be destroyed. Should you not comply, we will come in with our military and take back our land. Please consider. By stepping down, you will save thousands of lives and property from being destroyed." The queen asked the Russian ambassador to wait outside while she talked it over with her staff.

After a short discussion, the Russian was called back in, and the queen said, "For the safety of my people, I will step down. I'm sure our country will be in good hands with Igor and Roseanna leading them."

The following day, the queen went on TV and radio and informed the citizens of her decision. Some were happy and some were not.

Conclusion

$\mathcal{P}$ete and Judy returned to the family hotel where they were welcomed with open arms.

They stayed, as Judy worked in the billing and account department, while Pete worked with his parents in the administration branch. Joe and Bernadette took over her family's business in Florida, as her parents took over the London company. Margaret and the general stayed in Russia, traveling back and forth to Florida. Over the years, Pete and the queen had two sons — Pete and Joseph — and a daughter — Melissa.

Charlie and Connie had a daughter, Jennifer.

Joanne and Jerry had three sons — Jerry Junior, Michael, and Christopher.

Joe and Bernadette had two sons and a daughter — Joseph, Katherine, and Michael.

Candy and James had a son — Pete James — and two daughters — Dorothy and Joan.

Pete James joined the Green Berets. He wanted to be like Uncle Pete. Do you think his mother gave him her pin?

Judy took four items from the palace — what would you take?

The safe in the secret room was never opened — would you open the safe?

To My Sisters and Brothers of the Military

*D*uring my long life, which I hope will be much longer, I have met many military sisters and brothers. They would say I'm a veteran, but I never fought in a war.

I'm here to say that it doesn't matter. You were still willing to give your life for your country. You didn't go to Canada or get married or run off to some college. You answered the call when your country wanted you.

This is My Story

On June 19, 1966, I was to be married. Instead I was pledging my life to our country and becoming a member of the United States Army.

I was sent to Fort Gordon in Georgia where I was trained to be a soldier. It turned out that I an expert sharpshooter. Right before finishing basic training, I was told I was going to being trained as a sniper, but for whatever reason half my outfit came down with pneumonia. I believe it was the five mile hike we did in the pouring rain. Once out of the hospital, I could not continue my training, so I was sent to Fort Story to train on boats. I really did not know what the program was, but as we all know, we have no choice.

Long story short, I was trained to drive various vessels. Not too bad. I and my friend, another expert rifleman, graduated at the top of our class. My friend Dave and I received orders for Germany. While we were congratulating ourselves, the sergeant came over and crossed out 'Germany' and put 'Vietnam', while saying that, where I was going, he only wanted the best.

We were to report to Fort Dix in three days. I told the Sarge that I had not seen my girlfriend since I had entered the Army. He replied, "If she loves you, she will wait."

I did get to see her on my way for a few hours, but they felt like minutes.

We landed up in Long Bin. That night we had incoming mail. It was addressed to whoever was in camp. It did not care if you were a cook or clerk. Whoever received the mail cashed in their check. The Sarge saw our medals on our dress uniforms, handed us a rifle, and we went into the bush looking for them. We did not find them.

The next day, Dave and I were standing in Cam Rahn Bay, and Sarge was happy to see us. He gave us our assignments. We had the privilege of carrying five tons of explosives from ship to shore. I carried to the 5th division Green Berets. For safety reasons, I never carried a gun, but I did have support from the air.

When I came in after a long day, the cooks always put something aside for us, and the clerk always had our paperwork ready. After 11 months, 29 days, and the loss of many boats, I went home without firing a shot.

To me anyone who is or was in the military is a veteran.

If you want to know more, read my book, *A Gang Members Tale*.

Thank you, Wolfie

Veteran Crisis Line
800-273-8255